Rainbow and Sunshine

The compelling untold love story reveals the real bond of Honey and Moon whose premeditated engagement is a gateway to their destiny in their previous incarnation in which they swore to live to love each other in Oracle of Delphi. Being reborn after 5000 years they realize and reach their destiny in Delphi.

Contents

Celebration

The dining lounge of Jahangir House was a spectacular sight to marvel at. All the guests; relatives, business friends and acquaintances of Mr. Jahangir Khan's were invited to dinner that night. His family members were going to host the engagement party of his only daughter, Hunaina Khan, who was an apple of everyone's eye. Jahangir's mother called her Honey, for she thought her grand daughter was sweetest of all her grand children. Jahangir's family was comprised of his mother, whom every one called *Amma*, his wife, Tina, his only daughter, Honey and his late brother's daughter, Sweety. Jahangir's family belonged to an elite class in society. His house was a grand villa situated at the main drag in the middle of Crescent Town. Although he was a sophisticated man of society, he was every inch a traditional man. He had no personal friends except for Mr. Tabreiz Khan who lived abroad. Tabreiz was from Jahangir's community and they both were always fast friends. He had a small family of his wife Rose and his only son Mehroze in Toronto, Canada. Jahangir and Tabreiz had decided to turn their friendship into relationship many years before. It was now that their promise was materializing. Jahangir's daughter was being engaged to Tabreiz's son.

Jahangir House was adorned with fairy lights and high-powered fancy illumination from the rooftop to the main gate. All driveway was red carpeted. The red carpet was decked with colossal pots brimming over with fresh rose petals that gave off pleasant fragrance to mark the welcome ceremony. The lawn close to the driveway was occupied with dining tables and chairs at one side and barbeque set up at the other side. Gul, the family butler, was seen around at the front of the villa, giving out orders and tasks to his subordinates.

The lounge on the ground floor was crammed full of guests and hosts. Young girls, dressed up in bridal outfits, were singing local songs to every one's liking. Upstairs, the first storey contained five rooms around the lounge which had a thin passage in the center leading to a large terrace covered with glass.

The terrace looked onto the spacious lawn which was a family spot in the mornings and evenings.

Amma in her bright green *ghrara* was wondering if everything was perfectly ideal for the ceremony. She was happy and unhappy both, for she had an idea that Honey was not inwardly pleased with her engagement until she had acquired full understanding of her fiancé. Making her way into Honey's room, *Amma* patted her shoulder lovingly when Honey was closing her conversation on call. She looked over and faced her grandmother.

"You know I am not willing to accept dad's decision of my engagement, but I am taking it just for granted."

Honey aired her grievance, looking at her grandmother's face with love.

"I want you to be happy with your life partner. You know parents never make wrong decisions for their children." Amma assured her, cupping her face affectionately.

The guests were pouring in bringing presents when Mr. Tabreiz Khan, Mrs. Tabreiz Khan and Mehroze arrived in Jahangir House. The loud announcement was made of a warm welcome of the long awaited distinguished guests. Tabriez embraced Jahangir impatiently and emotionally. Rose and Tina joined their cheeks and hugged each other elegantly. Rose kissed Amma, asking after her and congratulated her on her grand daughter's engagement. Mehroze who was stout, chubby and unattractive young man followed his parents. He greeted Jahangir's family and received oodles of blessings and wishes.

Hunaina Khan was brought down to the lounge which was redolent with laughter, clamour and bonhomie. Mehroze was very curious to steal a glance at his fiancée. He was a very simple and traditional boy. He was always more than willing to accept his parents' decisions. This time he was exceedingly excited to see his would-be life partner. Hunaina, accompanied by Sweety, paced inch by inch closer to the cheering crowd who were enthusiastic about this sight of union. Mehroze fixed his eyes on Hunaina, holding his breath and feeling overjoyed at such a beautiful girl entering his life.

Tabreiz nudged Mehroze to close up on Hunaina for a photograph session.

Mehroze moved up and whispered to Hunaina, "H-e-l-l-o! Nice t-o m-e-e-e-t you!" She was shocked to hear his stammering. She looked up at her fiancé only to find a round-faced foolish stammerer. She looked puzzled, but answered his greeting gently. In no time, photographers made their presence felt instructing the couple to move closer to each other for the ring-wearing ceremony. Mehroze picked out the engagement ring of the fancy box and held Hunaina's right hand gently before shooting camera men. The ornate ring was slid through Hunaina's middle finger amid applauses and cheers. They looked at each other with intimate smiles.

Both families exchanged wishes with each other. Hunaina was still enraged at not having been filled in on such a serious problem. She had soon improved her outlook not betraying her feelings before a large crowd and keen photographers. Amma and Tina touched Mehroze's head for blessings and Jahangir thrust himself into his son in law-to-be. Rose kissed Hunaina's forehead and Tabreiz put his hand over her head as if he had found his lost daughter.

The engaged couple was showered with presents and gifts by eager guests in a bee line while Sweety was jostling through them for her photograph with her cousin. She got onto stage and shook hands with Mehroze and Hunaina. She introduced Sweety to her fiancé.

"Meet my cousin, Sunaina Khan." He smiled, "Nice to see you!"

Sweety looked at him intently as if she had seen him somewhere before. She burst, "You are in the stars!" Her puzzled expression looked weird to the couple, even she did not know what she had said. Hunaina stared at her with disapproval. Sweety was momentarily wondering why she had passed a foolish remark which was in the back of her head. But she did not bother her head over that trifle and took to the floor.

Orchestra came into action, the party lights were put on and she began to dance in accompaniment with her friends. The dance beats were followed by her song.

"Love and life are forever.

Moon and sun go together.

My sweet heart is bright.

Beloved ones are tried.

Love and life are forever."

Her song was heard with claps and whistles.

The Secret

Following the party both friends had a short conversation and Mr.Tabreiz took leave of Mr. Jahangir. Back at home Tabreiz wished to sound out his wife, Rose, and his son, Mehroze, about their interaction with Jahangir's family. Rose was so overjoyed at her bonding with Jahangir's family that she would not stop speaking highly of them. She went on talking about all family members one by one.

First, Rose commented on Amma's hospitality and Tina's taste for trendy clothes. Next, she spoke volumes about her would be daughter in law. She was highly complimentary about Hunaina's outlooks and manners. She even liked Sweety, the daughter of late Dilawer Khan's. She spent nearly half an hour talking out all the family members. Tabreiz had no option but to listen to her since she was the lady of the house. Taking his chance he turned to Mehroze, asking him about all Jahangir's family members.

"What is your opinion of them?" He inquired of his son, raising one of his eyebrows in pride.

"I have liked them all, *Baba*, but, I had an embarrassment when Hunaina disapproved of my spurious stammering. It was also embarrassing to hear her cousin say 'You are in the stars.' I didn't quite get what you had told me to fake this stammering for?"

Tabreiz stood up off the couch and came close to Mehroze. He seemed perturbed, sitting beside his son. He confirmed with his son's statement,

"Are you sure her cousin uttered,
'You are in the stars'?" Mehroze
looked at his father and said, "Yes!"
Tabreiz questioned again, "Are you
sure Sunaina said these words to
you?" The young obedient son
nodded. Tabreiz became occupied in
some deep thoughts and raised his
head from reflection. He began to
recount, "Moon, you know what? We
had left this ancestral house before
your birth. I was born here in Furjan.
While your mum was in the family
way, I had become a successful
astrologer. I knew that it was better
to move to Toronto, although Aga jee
and Bee jee did not agree to my
decision. They were right of their
own accord. This home was meant
for us. Aga jee was cross with me
because I was your grandfather's only
son and I wanted to take Rose away

from our hometown. I had to take this step for your safe birth. Aga jee and Bee jee were left alone, but your aunt, Mishi, my sister, came to live with them. They were happy, but they missed us more often. Anyway, I was on about your safe birth. As an astrologer I decided to name you Moon because it had some strong reason. Jahangir's wife, Tina, was also in the family way. According to astrology you and Honey were not to be born in the same town. Either you could have died or she could have died. Your lives were already interconnected. I had never believed in superstitions, myths and horoscopes till my Reverend brought me around them. He was my spiritual guide who had taught me Reiki and Astrology. I was advised to raise you away from Furjan where Jahangir lived too. My Reverend had a great insight into Astrology and Palmistry. He had said that you were being born the second time and so was Jahangir's daughter. It was too ludicrous to accept, but because Jahangir was his closest disciple and he was my teacher too, I came to believe him. You and Hunaina have been reborn. I asked you to fake stammering so that she wouldn't like you. According to my Reverend's prophesy you both will be happy and safe as soon as she picks you out by chance and calls up her previous incarnation." Tabreiz looked over at the large portrait of his spiritual teacher mounted on the wall. His attention to Mehroze was distracted by two cups of hot tea served by Rose who interposed herself between them eagerly.

"Your *Baba* is absolutely right." She added a remark to start her long-winded monologue, but her son put in a question to Tabreiz, "What does it have to do with her cousin's mention of the stars?" He asked curiously. Tabreiz went on, "This sentence is the reminder to your previous birth and it tells you to be ready for your confrontation to the impending doom. It simply suggests that Sunaina has been reborn too and she has warned you off coming close to Hunaina. She should have been your enemy in previous incarnation."

"I don't believe in it. How can a person be born again according to Science?" Mehroze whispered, not letting his father know what he opined. Rose was watching his puzzled expressions on his face. She wanted to change the topic.

"By the way, did you like Honey?" She blurted.

"Yes, mum! But I'm not much comfortable. I think she has not got a good impression of me." He answered.

Tabreiz laid his hand gently on Mehroze's shoulder. "You and Hunaina have never met before. It is your first visit home. We have returned to Dubai after 21 years. You've never seen her before and nor has she, so it's natural. Whatsoever you both will be happy together and we know it. The words of our Reverend will not be void." He assured his son.

"How was your Reverend sure we were reborn? I mean what's the proof?" Mehroze sounded puzzled.

Tabreiz and Rose exchanged looks with each other and Rose took her turn to speak. She stepped up close to her son, recalling that warning night . "It was a stormy night and your *Baba* and I were in Jahangir's house for dinner. His spiritual teacher was invited too. We were talking of the violent storm when Mr.Corum told us of strange signs in the sky. Meanwhile, Tina and I felt pains. He related those signs to your reincarnation. He told us to split up before your birth and Hunaina's birth. Both of you were to be born in different lands according to Mr.Corum. We didn't believe in all that account till we saw for ourselves the distant shooting stars in the raging storm."

In Jahangir House, all family members were still up chatting away, eating desserts and singing songs. Honey was not much happy because she could not find an ideal life partner in her fiancé. She was in her room having got changed. Sweety was somewhat confounded as to what her words had meant for her cousin's fiancé. She was still tracing her words before Honey. It did not bother Honey at all, but the most agonizing feeling was the fact that she had been engaged to a stout stammerer she had never seen before. She dismissed Sweety's idle chatter and decided to sleep.

Downstairs, sitting beside Tina in the lounge Jahangir asked her about all the arrangements and guests. Tina answered his queries, but she wanted to change the subject and talk out something about Honey. Her husband noticed that she was rather perplexed. He moved up to Tina and began to confirm if she was perturbed. He held her hand gracefully in his, looking at her face, which made her look more uncomfortable.

"Are you keeping something back from me, sweetheart?" He demanded.

"The words of your Reverend sometimes frighten me. His warnings and prophesies sound weird. I mean he said my recurring dreams of Honey in my pregnancy were the omen for her rebirth."

"Come on! Tina! It's a trivial matter. Don't worry! Our Honey will be happy with Mehroze."

"I pray everything go well. Honey and Mehroze are made for each other." She sounded less anxious. Jahangir's words assured her that she should be gratified.

"By the way, is he a stammerer? Honey is really concerned for him." She expressed her reservation.

"Not at all, Tabreiz and I have decided to obey our Reverend's instructions. She shouldn't like him at once. Honey has to pursue her destiny. Mehroze and Honey are the couple of the Divine decree." He clarified to Tina.

Zaaviyaar's rage

The following day both cousins went about their business. Their university fellows called for a super celebration of Honey's engagement. Their department and friends were so elated for her that they made a bee line to offer their congratulations. Sweety had to repeat herself to almost everyone, giving the full account of the event. Honey was inundated with hearty wishes too.

Their department was already adorned with festive ambience and crowded with friends when one of their friends shouted, "Happy engagement! My dearest and nearest Honey", from the door. He rushed into the packed room pushing others to reach his beloved friend, Honey. "Thank you so much, my prince!"

"Happiness in marriage is a chance of luck." He whispered in her ear, hugging her with warmth.

"What a warning? Zaar!" She uttered softly, still gathered in his embrace.

"I want to see you happy." Zaaviyaar looked into Honey's eyes closely, as if hypnotizing her.

Honey pulled herself away from his grip all of a sudden and engaged with other friends. Zaaviyaar turned to Sweety, talking of their upcoming study trip to Greece.

After a busy day, Zaar and Honey went for a short walk in the University Park. She looked at him and said, "I know you like me and you aren't pleased with my father's decision."

"I can't be a loser. Tell your dad to call off your engagement. It is a wrong decision." He blustered.

"I can't go against his will. He will never change his decision. You know him." She pleaded.

"Your father does not know me. My princess! I have never lost anything in my life."

"Let's close this topic! By the way, what about our upcoming project trip?"

"Next month! To Delphi, Greece!"

Honey smiled at her friend's update and they went on walking silently. It was not too late that Sweety joined in with them in the park as usual.

GOSSIPS

At home *Amma* was conversing with Mehroze when Honey arrived. Gul, the butler, reported to *Amma* that Honey was at the main-gate. She patted Mehroze on his shoulder and strolled off upstairs gracefully. Honey entered the lounge and looked at her stout and heavy weight fiancé with respect.

"Hi, how are you?" She greeted Mehroze.

"I'm good. How are yoou, H-oney?" He replied. His eyes were fixed on his fiancée as if he had been waiting to see her. Words seemed to have lost him.

"I am cool, Mehroze! How long have you been here?"

"For an hour! We're g-oing bback to C-a-n-a-daa to-m-orr-ow. I w-a-n-ted to see you and bid yoo fare-wel."

"Did you like our family?"

"Yes, very much!"

"Wh-ere are yoo ccoming f-rom?"

"From my university, it was a gathering with friends." She answered softly in a low tone.

"You are beautiful! Honey" He voiced his heart naturally, looking at her closely.

"Thank you! Mehroze" She smiled.

"I will w-a-n-t to bear all your ex-pen-ses now. Please do not re-fuuse me my due." He implored her.

She gazed at him a little and blushed at his request. "As you wish!" She nodded.

She sat down on a sofa beside him. A large tray full of refreshment was brought to the center table for him. He asked his fiancée to join in with him, which she accepted with a delight. They both had refreshment accompanied by tea together and then Mehroze left with a sweet sorrow of parting.

Honey's mind was soon distracted to their preparation for the trip to Greece. But the first and foremost formality was asking her father's permission which was as hard as drawing water from the well. Sweety made the first move to ask her uncle's permission. Jahangir and Tina were not satisfied at her explanation.

Sweety suggested, "It will be kind of you to consider our project on Oracle of Delphi. Honey and I have been toiling away at it for months."

"It's not our custom to allow girls to go. I need some time." He said to Sweety.

"It will be too late, dad, I mean we have made all arrangements. This trip is next month. We have already filled you in on it and you have given your consent. Now we are confirming your permission. Please!" Honey pleaded with her father.

Jahangir relented and granted his permission for their trip. He put a condition that both the girls should be careful with their meals. They readily accepted it and ensured that their preparation was almost complete.

Sweety was too exhilarated to keep it to herself and she began to share it with their relatives. She wanted to call Mehroze to say that she and Hunaina were going on a university trip to Delphi. She felt a great attraction towards Mehroze. Her heart was growing fond of him imperceptibly although he was going to become a brother-in- law to her. She did not feel like talking out her deep feelings to anyone, even to Honey.

The phone call was soon made to Honey's fiancé who was in Toronto now. She told Mehroze of their project trip and had a chat with him.

Trip to Delphi

Jahangir, *Amma* and Tina saw them off at the airport with sincere wishes and domestic instructions. Both girls were brimming over with excitement when Zaaviyaar approached them in the departure lounge.

"Hey girls, sorry for coming late." He smiled rather sheepishly, shaking hands with them.

"It's alright! This is not the first time." Both remarked spontaneously gesturing him to sit beside them.

Jahangir's family had hardly got home when Mehroze called him on his cell phone. He picked up Mehroze's call to encourage him to reach Honey in Delphi, so that she could find her real soul mate in him.

The trio made their arrival in Delphi and proceeded to the nearest hotel in which their room had already been booked. Zaaviyaar was in the lead to check into.

He introduced himself to the reception, "Hello, I am Zaaviyaar Khan from Asr University, U.A.E. and these are my university fellows."

"Hello, Hunaina Khan!" She greeted.

"Sunaina Khan!" The latter also made her introduction to the receptionist.

The receptionist who was a young tall girl smiled at them, "You are welcome to Ritz Hotel. We are pleased to have you as our distinguished guests here. Your university has already informed us of your arrival. We wish you all the best for your archaeological project."

"Thank you so much! Nice talking to you." The three expressed their gratitude.

"By the way, I am Annie Maldonado. I am your host on behalf of my team. How was your flight?"

"It was great. We have enjoyed ourselves although my colleagues have run a mild temperature. We have come here by bus from Athens." Hunaina said gently.

"Let me show you your rooms!" The receptionist smiled again. She told porters to lug up their suitcases and luggage with care and led them up to their rooms, wishing them to have some rest.

Zaaviyaar and Sweety soon fell severely ill the next hour and stayed in their rooms. Hunaina got out of her room a little later feeling fresh.

She walked out to explore the town in the afternoon, carrying her hand camera since it was famous as the one of the most phenomenal touristy spots. Hunaina's heart was swelling with exuberance and pleasure as she advanced towards the Mount Parnassus. It was not long before she got to the exquisite cafe which was overcrowded with many tourists and visitors. She ordered coffee for herself and began to capture the picturesque sights of Parnassus, deciding where to look first and where to look next in the state of immense exhilaration and gratification when a handsome young boy in a fair complexion of her own age joined her at the coffee table.

"Hello! This is Moon." He held out his hand with a familiar look on his face.

"Hi! This is Hunaina." She looked up at him from her coffee cup, extending her hand. She noticed that this young man was no other than Mehroze. Her mind studied his outlook for a second.

"How is this coffee?" He enquired rather casually, as if wanting to strike a conversation with her.

"It's delicious and strong. You are Moon. Am I right?" She responded to him with a glee and reassured herself of his name.

"You're right! Do you know me?"

"Well, it's my fiance's name too and you look like him. Though he is plump and he stammers, he is just like you."

"What if I say you look like my fiancée and she is just like you?"

"What a coincidence? Lovely! Where are you from Mr. Moon?" She laughed.

"I am from Turkey. I love sightseeing. By the way, you are no less than this beauty of Parnassus." Moon sighed and moved his head around.

"Are you serious? Or are you flirting with me?"

"Do you see flirt in my eyes? In my words?"

"By the way, I'm going ahead. Thank you for company!"

"It's going to be evening soon. You'd better go back. If you wish to know more of me, come over to my lodge."

"Where are you staying?"

"Bianca Lodge, room number 42."

"Let's see next time! Thanks for your advice!"

Her chance meeting with Moon kept troubling her mind in her hotel room. She was wondering what to do to confirm if it was someone else. She had even changed the sim on her hand phone without saving Mehroze's contact number. She did not go to bed till late at night. Sweety and Zaaviyaar were not active and awake. The idea of confirming that strange young man's identity with her cousin was only possible when Sweety was up and willing.

The next morning was not good for both of her traveling partners since their health was deteriorating. Hunaina and the hotel manager arranged for a doctor's visit to their rooms and they were checked up. They had caught some unknown weather allergy which had to last a few days. A complete bed rest and proper medication were prescribed, which was undertaken by Ritz management with courtesy.

It was a broad daylight at noon, which made her go out into the town to explore more of Parnassus and even capture the heartening sights that were the grandeur of Delphi. She made her way to the same cafe and looked around to see the horde of tourists. She sat at the table, waiting for her order to come when Moon joined her again with a smile.

"We are destined to see more of each other." He greeted Honey warmly, sipping his coffee.

She smiled back at him, "It figures! By the way, have you been following me?"

"I don't know. I think you have been following me because I am having coffee before you. What about a hike?"

"Sure! I'd love it, but just wait till I finish my coffee." She giggled with delight.

In no time, Moon and Honey went for a pleasure walk. Honey was deeply touched by his words and presence. While they were walking, their gazes met in silence more often. It was the most pleasant opportunity for him to sing a lovely song. He held her hand dearly as she was about to slip on the slope of the mountain and told her to be careful. Honey thanked him, feeling obliged, to which he responded in a song, "Having you close to my side is my pride.

Come and say you will be my bride. Bringing me all the happiness on a hike, don't step aside.

We will love each other forever and will never hide."

She could not understand why his song worked on her mind and soul imperceptibly and why she could not resist his invitation to friendship in spite of her engagement to Mehroze who was not possibly Moon to the best of her knowledge. She kept hiking along the gigantic mountain, holding onto Moon till Oracle came into sight. The couple halted at the sight of this Oracle of Delphi which seemed very familiar to them both. They inched on forward to approach this ancient site whose imposing structure and classical architecture charmed them and they gravitated towards this temple. The exterior walls inscribed with ancient Grecian characters captured their memory as they approached them. Honey felt that she had belonged to this land before. Moon felt that he had once been here before. All of a sudden, the wind blew strongly through the majestic temple which reminded them of their previous incarnation.

Honey began to remember her first life slowly. The images of a royal place, queen, princess, a young gladiator stained with blood flitted across her mind. The wind was still blowing furiously while pandemonium broke out and all the other people cleared out.

"What's this happening?" Moon coughed.

"I think it's going to be a storm." Honey guessed.

"It is your welcome to Oracle of Delphi, Princess Honey and Emperor of Rome." Said a strange old man who was standing close to them. His voice sounded familiar to them. He was dressed in a long black coat and he held a staff for support. He was a superannuated man with a wizened and wrinkled body. His deep seated eyes had an extraordinary shine that had a special meaning. His white hair and facial features were suggestive of his endurance and wisdom.

"Who're you?" They inquired curiously.

"Pollo, from ancient Greece, 5000 B.C. when you both lived for each other." The old man whined. He had tears in his eyes.

"I can remember somewhat, I might have been the princess of Greece and you were my counsellor." She murmured.

"We loved each other, I was from Rome. Am I right?" Moon sounded inquisitive.

"Yes, Greece and Rome were the most powerful countries then. You were the step younger sister of the ruling queen, Sunain. And you were the emperor of Rome when Sunain and Honey visited Rome first time. You were known to be the best gladiator and swordsman of the time." He satisfied Moon's curiosity.

"It may be right. But why have you fooled me into thinking you were someone else, not my fiancé. It has only just become clear to me." She moved up to Moon and looked into his eyes.

"How have you got to know now?" He was surprised.

"She has picked you out by destiny here." The old man answered.

"I have got you. We both loved each other. But I can't believe we were separated." Honey mumbled to herself.

"You both vowed to live together and die together. The queen and that villain had you separated. But see The Almighty has brought you back."

"But what had happened? Please tell us everything!" They synchronized.

5000 B.C.

The old man looked at Moon and Honey and began to tell them, "The amphitheater of the capital was honoured with the Greek queen and her younger sister to sight the Roman gladiator. Spectators were cheering, clapping and shouting when he took to the field. His sword was high up in his hand, but his eyes and ears were set on every move the lions were making. The show was the combat between life and fierce death.

Both the beasts were running at him wildly, instilling fear in hearts and souls of the spectators, clouding dust and roaring like thunder as he stood before them fearless with a sword in his hand. In the blink of an eye, the attack was mounted, but the swiftest sweep of his sword and deepest drive of his dagger sent them off wounded. The beasts were more enraged. The next move was being awaited when he and they both lunged forward at each other and the former shot his spears into their heads.

His victory was outstanding and unmatched. People were spellbound by his unprecedented valour once he waved his spears. The Greek princess who was seated high above beside her queen sister suddenly shouted at the top of her voice, "Watch out for him!" He turned around like flash stabbing his wounded attacker whose jaws sprinkled blood all over him.

That gladiator was the Roman emperor, Moon and the Greek princess was Honey. She rushed down to congratulate the victor insanely when her queen was lost in his love. She said to me, "Pollo! Stop Honey reaching him." I ran after her, but to no avail.

The whole theatre was amazed to see her approach him. He saw her and said, "Thank you for saving my life!" She breathed heavily, "Next time you will save my life. We will be quits with each other."

"I will visit your country, dear princess!"

"My pleasure! I will wait for you."

I begged her to return to her queen who was green with envy above. She decided to arrange for an extravagant treat in Greek to which the Roman gladiator was cordially invited. In fact, it was the formal welcome to Roman emperor as a token of friendship between two great countries at that time.

The emperor, Moon, returned their visit and Greece gave him and his two men a warm welcome. He was introduced to the strongest man of then Greek army, Zaar, who was considered the most powerful general.

"You are welcome here!" Sunain greeted the emperor.

"I am privileged to be here." He thanked the queen.

"Meet our most powerful man, the general of our Greek army, Zaar."

"I am not impressed. Rather, I am impressed with the most beautiful woman of Greek empire."

"Thank you! I am sure you will always be impressed with me."

"I beg your pardon! I mean the princess to be the most beautiful woman of Greece. Where is she?"

"What? Oh! I see! Honey is here."

The queen and her general were greatly embarrassed and irked by the words of their visitor. The emperor, Moon, was soon introduced to the beautiful and graceful young princess who was summoned from her chamber. She smiled at the bold emperor and fell in love with him the moment he looked deep into her eyes. The envious queen and Zaar received the emperor of Rome and his two loyal men into their palace under protocol. The Roman hero was served a sumptuous dinner in the presence of Sunain and Honey. He was more attentive to the princess at dinner, which was noticed by her elder sister. Honey asked him to dispense with formalities and her kind nature encouraged him to ask her hand in marriage.

"Your highness, I am highly grateful for your generosity and hospitality!" He expressed.

"You are most welcome! My counterpart! I wish you to call me by my name. We are equal in rank and honour." Sunain voiced her dearest wish.

"I will be humbled if you will accept my proposal for marriage."

Her face turned white and she called out my name in exasperation. I had already judged what was likely to happen. She ordered me to bring

Honey's syrup for epilepsy. The syrup was administered to the princess before the honourable visitor to assure him that appearances can be deceptive.

"Dear emperor! With all due regard, I can not accept your proposal for marriage to Honey because our princess has a sleeping sickness. Until she is cured of it, we will not consider any proposal."

"I can cure her of it. Nature has plenty of energy that will help her shake it off. I am a therapist."

"For your kind information she is still under treatment at the hands of Pollo."

"But the princess has not yet recovered fully. My treatment is the power of energy in nature. I wager that your beloved sister will heal in a trice."

"She has been suffering from it ever since she was a child. I challenge you to cure her within three days. If you win this challenge, I will approve of your proposal for marriage."

"I accept your challenge. Honorable queen! She will be with me for these three days and I will take her out into the fields in the broad sunlight for treatment."

"I agree, but her counsellor, Pollo, will be with you."

"Thank you! Your highness!"

Honey was most pleased with this method of treatment because she was never allowed to go outdoors. She was also pleased with Moon's attention to her.

The next morning we ambled down to the open valley. She held his hand gently and said, "Thank you for helping me, Moon! I love you. I wish to marry you and live with you all my life."

"I will not take any 'thank you' from you now. Give smiles! You are very beautiful, Honey. You look even more beautiful when you smile. Never stop smiling. You are my first love and I promise we will be wedded."

He ran her through the wide fields where Honey felt at ease. The sights breathed vivacity into her to sing loudly. She danced across the green valley, looking over at the high mountains, tall trees and nearest temple. Her happiness knew no bounds, for she thought she was free to enjoy herself.

Moon asked her to seat herself on a low hillock which was the right spot for his method of treatment for her sleeping sickness. She was positioned in the direction of the sun and her head was screened with his hands for a little while. Then her head was exposed to the sun again. This performance was repeated three times before me. Honey was receiving this treatment patiently and quietly, but her bright eyes were still expressing gratitude for his treatment.

This practice lasted for the other next two mornings. Meanwhile, the queen was certain that her step sister would not be cured fully, for she thought that the emperor's therapy was almost ineffective.

She wished to talk to her distinguished guest, Moon, about her challenge. The emperor appeared before the queen to fill her in on his successful experiment which brought out the worst in her.

"How is it possible? We cannot believe it."

"Your highness! It is possible. Your princess has healed now. You can see for yourself."

"We will see for sure! Honourable emperor!"

It was an unbelievable truth that the princess had been cured of epilepsy when it came to testing her. But it infuriated the queen immensely. She had never loved her stepsister in life. What she wanted was the throne of Greece for herself and then the throne of Rome. She was reminded of her word that was almost impossible to ignore.

"Now you have even tested your princess and confirmed that she has been relieved of her chronic illness, you are requested to honour your promise."

"My dear counterpart! We have found her better and acknowledged that your challenge has really worked wonders for her, but accepting your marriage proposal for Honey, now, will be too early to decide. We still do not know if she has recovered forever. Even, this acceptance of proposal may cause some problems for you later."

"Honourable queen! Your word is your bond and if your memory serves you well, you did not put any procrastination in consideration. Furthermore, you have called for and consulted prominent healers on her full recovery after my therapy and they have asserted that your princess has fully recovered. As far as I am concerned, I will always be thankful that Honey is my soulmate."

"You are in the stars. You accept the consequences of this marriage."

Their marriage was decided finally. Sunain was not pleased with this announcement, although she had given her consent. Another person who was jealous of their love and marriage was Zaar. He confided to me that he had been longing to get the beautiful princess for himself. He was so worst with envy that he wanted to assassinate the Roman emperor in our land. I exerted myself to appease his wrath, but I knew what he could do next. Honey was overjoyed at her new life, brimming over with ecstasy and elation she could not help flaunting her love of Moon. She came to his chamber with me two days before their departure from Greece.

"I have something to talk about."

"You are most welcome to talk to me, dear princess."

"I have always been thinking I am unfortunate. You will be surprised to hear that when I was born my mother died giving birth to me. My father's first wife who was my elder step-sister's mother raised me along with her own daughter. The Greek king was too occupied in his state matters to spend time with me. My step mother also passed away when I was young and my father's demise followed hers soon after. My elder sister ascended to the throne. I rattled around this lonely palace miserably. I became sick, but my counsellor looked after me as my father. I would have died otherwise. I wish that Pollo stayed with us in Rome after our marriage. Will you honour my request?"

"Your wish is my command. Pollo will live with us in Rome. Are you happy?"

"I am more than happy."

The day before their departure we visited this Greek temple. I prayed for their eternal union and they prayed for my long life. Moon thanked me for being with them. But, I did not deserve to be thanked because I had been chosen as an assassin.

On the fateful day, the emperor of Rome, his bride- to- be, his two loyal men and I set off from Greece. The couple was ecstatic about their new home and life. Our voyage on *Angaria* was different as the violent storm engulfed us on the troubled water. Moon was still studying the raging storm and the horrendous lightning across the red sky and his men were helping me with erecting masts and sails. Honey was uneasy about the situation, as she had an Ill-boding feeling of some disaster. I was the wretched slave to the wicked queen and her general who had ordered killing them both in the name of elopement. I could not do anything to break myself free from my unwavering subservience to those lords who had already designed their fate. The heinous moment approached when Honey was saying, "We will never part from each other even if death comes our way." I closed in on her, drew out my dagger and plunged it in her back. She looked around and saw my face with a smile. Moon gathered her into his strong arms, calling out her name and eyeing me vengefully. I hung my head in shame before him.

"Moon, I am yours forever, but promise not to kill Pollo. I will come for you again."

He pulled out the dagger of her back and threw it down, shouting out to his men to arrest me. He did not know that his two guards had been bought over by the queen. I picked it up when he turned his back on me and ran it through him. He turned around in agony to me and both his men held him down so I could attack him over and over till he was killed. He fell close to Honey and breathed his last.

"My beloved, see, I did not kill Pollo. I will come for you again."

Their assassination and blood subdued the storm which had witnessed my betrayal and butchery.

I never returned to Greece. Instead, I had sent the two men to the queen with the message that both Honey and Moon had been murdered.

Later, Zaar killed both the men and captured Rome where Sunain ruled for years. The only aim in my life was to wait for you to come back for each other. I was sure that you would visit this Oracle where five thousand years ago I blessed your union."

Force of Karma

"It means Sweety and Zaar were our deadly enemies." Honey blabbered to herself.

"Of course, this is why I have given you this tracker-ring on our engagement for your location." Moon sighed in relief.

"It is my ring only that has brought you here. See, Pollo! My sweetheart has been following me by this ring, not by destiny." She blushed innocently.

The old wizened man smiled at her belonging to Moon. He held their hands and brought them close to him. "Honey and Moon have reunited today. My wish to see them together again has come true, my Lord."

Old Pollo shouted in joy and fell down dead. The couple let down to his body, calling out his name. Moon felt his pulse, examined his retina and picked him up with his fiancée behind him. They were offered help by other tourists who had joined in with them where the old man had died, but Moon dismissed them.

Moon and Honey rushed the wizened old dead man to the nearest town hospital. The hospital declared that the old man had just died naturally. Honey was still surprised at a series of strange events, though the new outlook of her fiancé was incredibly overwhelming. She was wondering how Mehroze could lose weight so quickly.

"I just don't get my head around how you slimmed down within a month."

She effused, resting her head onto Moon's shoulder.

"You were not in picture. Jahangir uncle and *Baba* had the knowledge of our rebirth. Uncle also knew you had to come here for your university project and he had already decided with *Baba* what to do. Our family engagement ceremony, my clumsy look, my stammering were planned. Their spiritual teacher had told them we were made for each other, but you should pick me out somewhere else. I am like this. I put on to discourage you liking me. I am a Reiki specialist, so it didn't take me much time to slim down again." He said, patting her head lovingly. She raised her head and smiled at him. They enjoyed each other's company in the hospital lobby, waiting for the doctor.

In the meanwhile, Honey noticed that Sweety and Zaaviyaar were being stretchered away into the emergency department.

"Moon, let's go and see Sweety and my uni fellow." She shouted.

"Let's come! Don't panic! I am here." He comforted her. They followed the stretcher till the I.C.U. She checked up her hand phone on the silent mode only to find the messages from Ritz Hotel.

"Let me call home to tell mom and dad. What about Zaar's home?" She said to Mehroze.

"You had better call home. I will get his family's contact." He suggested to her.

He acquired Zaaviyar's phone from the hotel and called his family.

Half an hour later, the busy doctors emerged from the intensive care unit and declared that Sunaina and Zaaviyaar had expired. The news sent shivers down her spine. She could not believe her ears and began to cry for her cousin, Sunaina. Mehroze helped her out of the hospital and drove her to Ritz Hotel.

Mehroze calmed her down and explained to her that they were destined to die there. It was all the law of destiny. She now realized that her fiancé was right.

Within a few days, they returned to their counties and Jahangir and Tabreiz congratulated each other. Finally, the wedding was held in Furjan, binding Honey and Moon to live together forever.

Faizan Akhter

Love is life and life is love!

Dear readers remember we are born to live for the search of true love.

Give your reviews of this book and connect with me.

Disclaimer

All names, characters, places and events in this novel are fictitious. Any resemblance to living or dead persons will be coincidental.

Faizan Akhter asserts the right to be the author and copyright holder of this work.